Sunday Comics

LARGE AND LOVABLE

MARMADUKE

Brad Anderson

TOR

A TOM DOHERTY ASSOCIATES BOOK

4

5

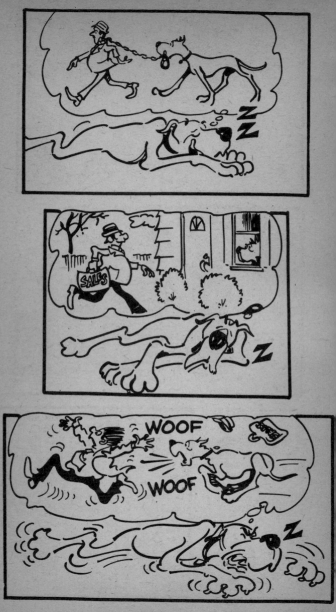

8

9

12

13

17

18

19

21

27

33

© 1980 United Feature Syndicate, Inc.

39

41

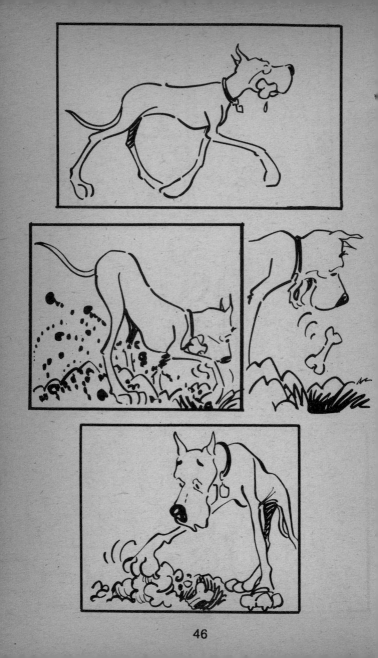

48

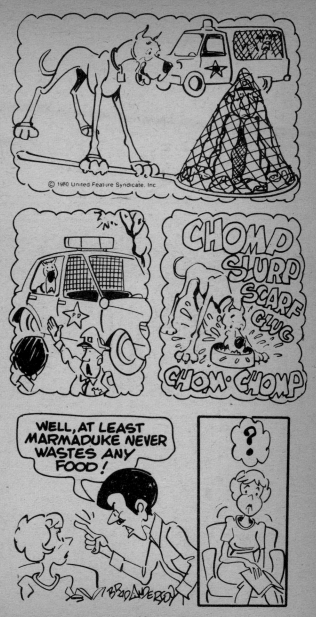

49

50

51

57

61

65

66

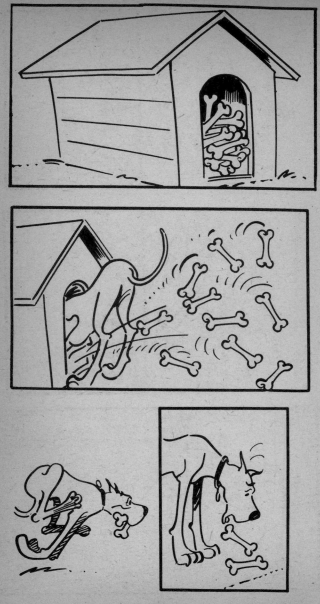

2-18

73

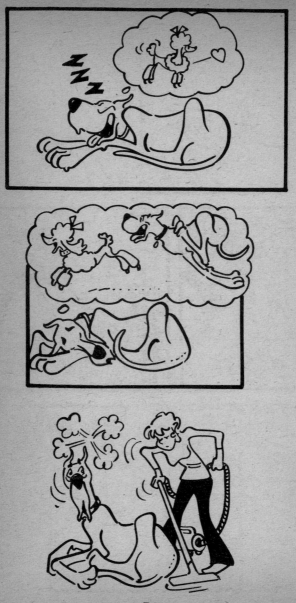

81

84

87

88

89

94

GROAN

104

107

110

111

114

118

119

121

126

© 1979 United Feature Syndicate, Inc.

132

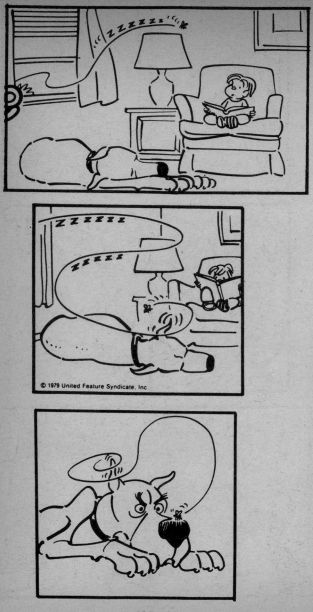

137

138

139

149

150

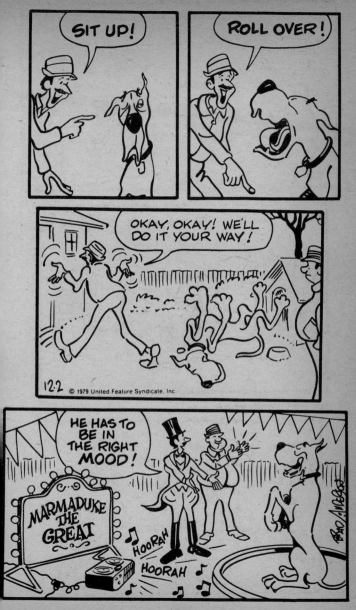

153

155

157

158

159

161

163

165

167

© 1978 United Feature Syndicate, Inc.

170

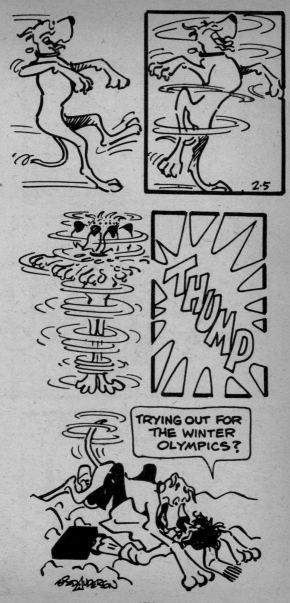

WOOF

181

189

195

201

211

212

215

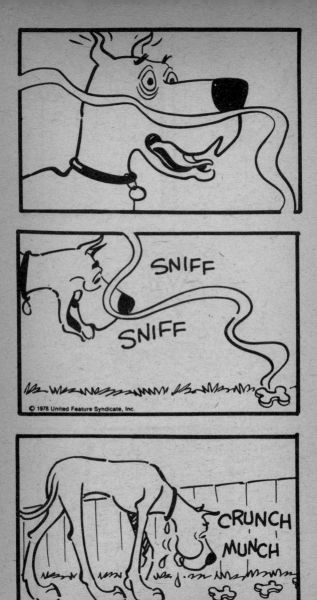

221

225

228

229

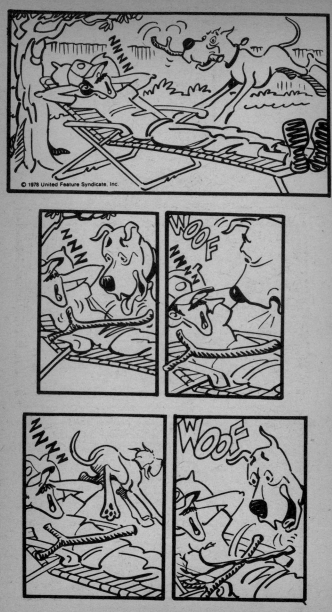

237

239

244

245

252

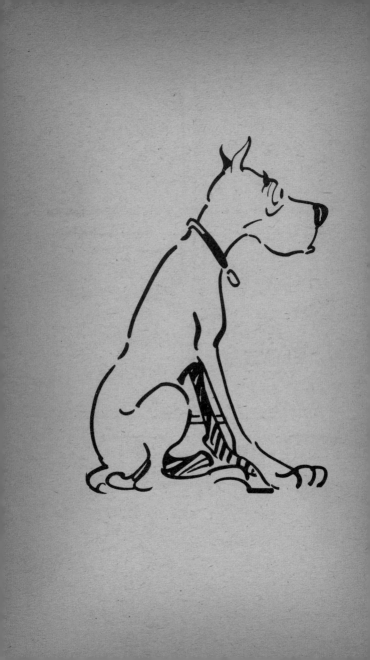